I0788378

The Hungry Crooks

Written by Petronella Schofield
Illustrated by Tenille Dowe

First Printing, 2025
Published by Creative Heart Connection
www.creativeheartconnection.com

ISBN: 978-1-7635928-9-6

To children everywhere

The Hungry Crooks

Written by Petronella Schofield

Illustrated by Tenille Dowe

I went into the garden -
the chooks were all out there.

I took a bowl of melon
and sat down on the chair.

The black chook eyed the melon.
Her eyes were brown and bright.

She flapped her wings and gave a squawk
then jumped with all her might.

She knocked the bowl out of my hands.
The melon hit the ground.

The black chook pecked
and gobbled fast.
The others gathered round.

They pushed and shoved,
and fought and pecked.

They scratched and clawed until they realised that the food was gone,
and then they all stood still.

The black chook looked at me again.
Her sharp eyes seemed to say.....

'We'd like some more.
That's not enough!
We want to eat all day!'

I sighed and got up
from the chair.

I went to go inside,
but Mum was coming
out the door.

'I've got some more!'
she cried.

We went into
the garden
and sat down
on the chair.

The chooks were
disappointed.......
They wouldn't get
their share.

We sat and ate our melon.
The chooks watched in dismay.
Their heads were cocked,
their beaks agape.

They wanted more that day.

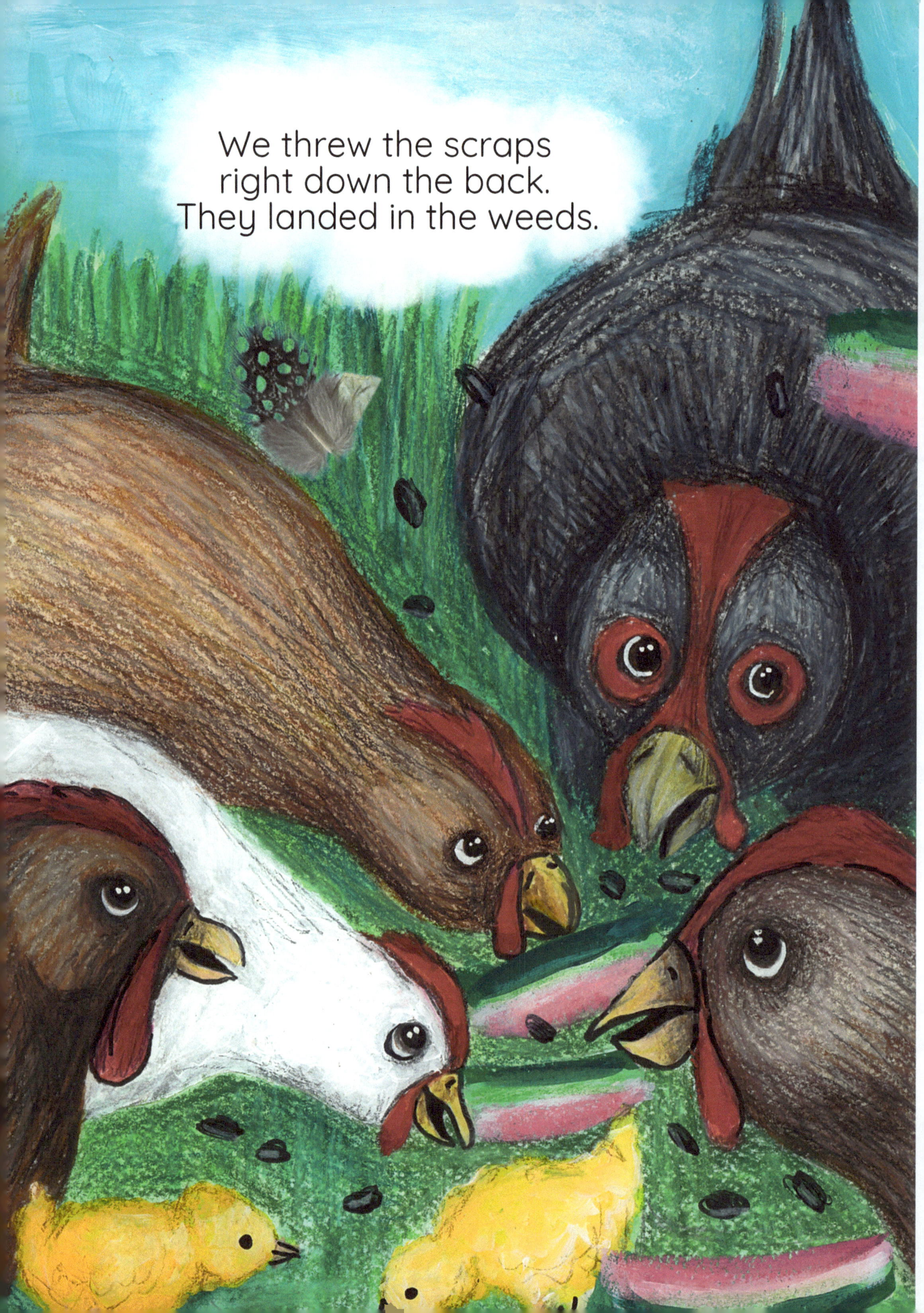

We threw the scraps
right down the back.
They landed in the weeds.

The chooks were happy
'cause they had the rind
and all the seeds.

If you go to the garden with food
you want to eat......

Beware of chooks,
the hungry crooks, with
beaks and springy feet.

The End